Chloe + Athena —
A real sea story from
a real sea captain!

[signature]
Nov '21

Compass Rose Press USA
Copyright © 2021 by Lew Maurer
All rights reserved.

No part of this publication may be reproduced, stored in or introduced into a retrieval system, or transmitted, in any form, or by any means (electronic, mechanical, photocopying, recording, or otherwise), without the prior permission of the publisher except in the case of brief quotations embodied in critical articles and review. Requests for permission should be directed to lew@compassrosepressusa.com.

Book Cover and Interior Design by Monkey C Media
Edited by Stephanie Thompson
Photos in the backstory from Shutterstock except where noted

First Edition 2021
Printed in the United States of America

ISBN: 978-1-7335150-2-3 (hardcover)
ISBN: 978-1-7335150-4-7 (ebook)

Library of Congress Control Number: 2021914831

Visit us at www.CompassRosePressUSA.com

Herman was tired of hiding.

"If only I could crawl down to the beach and play in the sand."

Just then, a shadow passed over and Herman quickly scurried back into the rocks.

"Peck, peck, peck!"

Herman knew that if he crawled out too far the gulls might dive down and eat him up. And during the night, when the tide comes in and the water rises up over the rocks, Herman had to hide from hungry fish too, especially the snappers. Snappers don't sleep at night and many little crabs get caught in their sharp teeth.

Herman often dreamed of leaving the rocks so he could see the rest of his island. He spent so much time off by himself, looking and thinking about it, that other crabs began to tease him. Some of them called him Herman the hermit.

He didn't like being teased.

At least I'm not the only one who has to hide, thought Herman.

The little fish had to hide from the big snappers too, and the mussels had to hide from the seagulls. Sometimes a seagull will find a mussel near the water and rip it off the rocks with its strong beak.

One time, when Herman was very young, he was almost eaten. A gull reached into his hiding place and grabbed Herman by his little claw. He held on tight with his other claw and when the gull tried to pull him out, his little claw popped right off.

Poor Herman!

Luckily for him, as he grew up, his claw grew back even bigger than before. He looked very strange with one regular-sized claw and one big claw. But it was bigger and stronger than the other crabs', and Herman was proud of his mighty claw.

Early one morning, a gull landed right above Herman's crack. Herman peered up. This gull did not make the usual scary, screeching noises.

Loud screeching is the gull's way of saying, "This is my rock! I am king of this rock!" And if another gull comes along, sometimes they fight over the rocks.

But this gull said nothing. She was a young gull, and very thin. Herman was careful not to move.

Herman saw that she was quite different than the other gulls. She was smaller, with darker colors, and black eyes. As he looked in her eyes he thought that she seemed sad.

Herman remembered when he lost his claw. She seemed different too, but he reminded himself that she was still a gull. So he didn't move.

Herman wanted to be brave, so in his biggest voice, said, "Hello, my name is Herman. I have never seen a seagull like you before. Where are you from?"

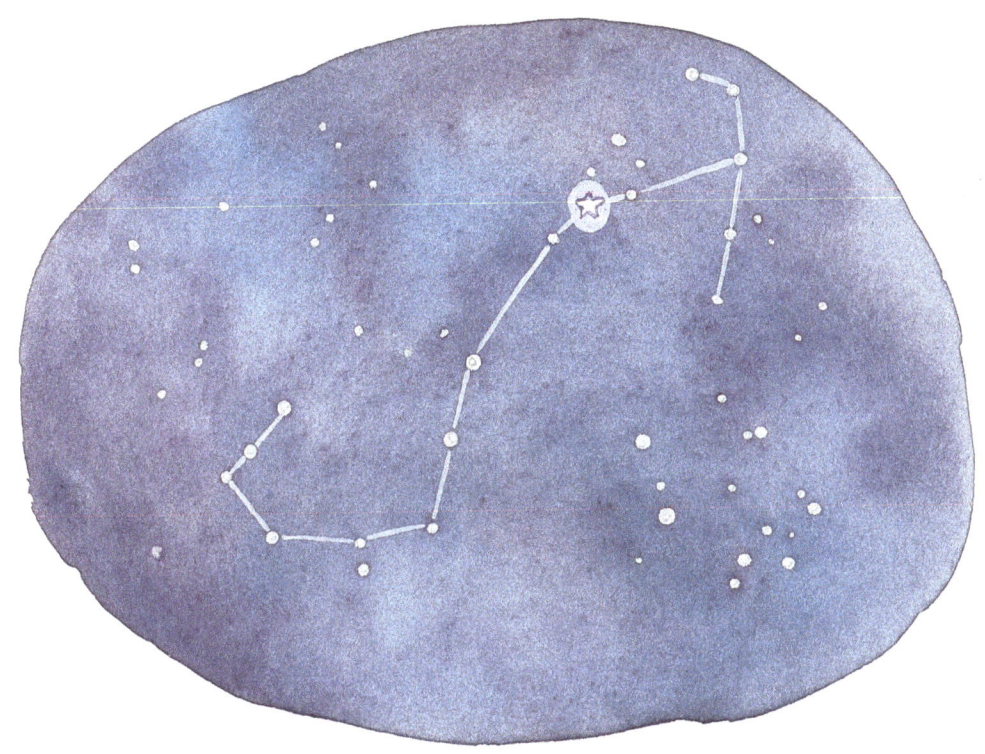

"My name is Antares. I am named after a star," she said. "My friends call me An, and I am the princess of my flock. One day, the water all around our island turned red and the fish swam away.

"I flew all day and all night to find blue water and fish for our babies. Although I was very tired, I wanted to return to my island with the good news.

"That night a terrible storm came. I flew as hard as I could, but the wind was too strong. I became so weak that I could barely fly any longer. Then, I saw this island and landed on your rock."

"Are you lost now?" Herman asked.

"No, I'm not lost," An replied. "I can use the sun and the stars to find my way home, but I'm too weak to fly. I'm too weak to even catch a fish."

Herman was afraid for the gull. She was the only gull who had ever talked to him. He did not want her to die. Then, he had an idea.

An was very surprised when Herman came out of his crack dragging a small mussel in his big claw. An could have easily eaten him up, but she didn't because he was her friend.

One after another, Herman brought many mussels to An. Herman was tired, but he was excited to be helping his friend and proud of his big, strong claw.

As the sun started to go down, Herman was near the water on the outside of the rocks. Suddenly a small wave splashed against the rock and Herman fell.

Waiting below was a big snapper. Herman closed his eyes and felt jaws grab his little body. He kicked and struggled, but he couldn't get free.

"Stop kicking so much, or I will drop you," scolded An. "I am still weak, but not too weak to help my friend."

For the first time in his life, Herman did not have to hide from the gulls. An was not only a princess, she was also a better flier than any of the big seagulls on his island. If any gull dared to come near his rock An would drive them away with her sharp beak and great speed.

Soon she was catching fish and back to her full strength.

"It's time for me to go home, little Herman."

"Antares," Herman said, "You are truly a princess. Thank you for being my friend."

"And you, Herman, are the true king of this rock."

"An," he said. "Could I ask you for one last favor? All my life I have dreamed of walking on the beach. Could you take me to the sand and watch over me while I have one little walk?"

Herman's heart was pounding as An flew high into the sky and did a few rolls and flips to give him a big thrill! When she put him down on the sand Herman was very dizzy. An laughed at how funny he looked as he ran around and around in circles.

And then, the most amazing thing happened. Herman came upon an old, empty shell. It was different than any he had ever seen at the rocks. It was a strong, thick shell. When he peeked in he found just enough room to wriggle inside.

"Why are you laughing?" An asked. "And what is that shell on your back?"

"My biggest wish in the whole world has come true," said Herman. "With this hard shell on my back, I can walk all over my island and nothing can eat me."

An pretended to peck at him. Not even the strongest gull could pull him out or crack his new shell.

"Good bye, my little king."

Herman sniffed. "Antares, whenever I look up at the night sky, I will find the star you are named for and I will remember my true friend, my very own princess."

And the princess gull flew home to her flock.

BACKSTORY

In nature, animals do not talk to each other like Antares and Herman, but many of the things in this story are interesting and true. In this story, Herman is a Land Hermit Crab. They live in rocks and on the beaches, near the ocean. As Hermit crabs grow, they must find larger and larger empty shells to use for protection. Sometimes, a large crab cannot find an empty shell large enough and they have to hide in rocks or even old seaweed on the beach. And they really do have one large claw, like Herman. When a Hermit crab is scared, they hide inside the shell and use their big claw like a shield, to cover them from animals that would like to eat them.

Hermit crab using a Turban Shell

Pacific Cubera Snapper

Snappers are large fish that live near rocks and like to feed at night. They eat all kinds of fish, crabs and other marine creatures. They have powerful jaws and sharp teeth. If a hermit crab falls into the water, the snappers can crush their shells or swallow them shell and all.

The seagulls are Herring Gulls. They are large gulls that make loud, screeching noises and fight over food every day. They will eat anything they can swallow, including crabs and fish. They fly high in the air sometimes and drop mussels and clams onto rocks to crack them open. And they do eat crabs if they catch them in the open.

Herring Gull

Antares is a Heermann's Gull. They are smaller than a Herring Gull, and more beautiful. They live along the southwest coast of North America and feed on small marine creatures and fish. They are better fliers than larger gulls, and known to steal fish from Brown Pelicans.

Heermann's Gull
Photo courtesy Christoph Moning

The star Antares is named for is a beautiful, reddish colored star in the constellation of Scorpius. It is classified a Red Supergiant because it is much larger than our sun, and one of the brightest stars in the night summer sky.

Antares star

The red water that came to Antares's island is called a plankton bloom. It is caused when very tiny ocean creatures called phytoplankton bloom, releasing toxins that kill fish and other marine life.

"Red Tide," or plankton bloom

Mussels, attached to rocks

The mussels are California Mussels. The strong fibers that hold them to the rocks are silk-like threads called byssus. It takes up to three years for a mussel to grow to adult size, about the length of a man's finger. Seagulls, fish, and even people love to eat the sweet meat inside.

AUTHOR

Growing up on fishing boats, the author has spent his entire life on the water, repairing, building, and operating commercial and pleasure vessels all over the world. This depth of knowledge and experience gave him the ability to build and captain Moana a very special, long-range power catamaran. His love affair with the sea is tangible as he describes in authentic detail, his fifteen-year odyssey to the most remote places on our planet. He calls San Diego home ... when he is home.

ILLUSTRATOR

Candace Camling lives in Des Moines, Iowa with her family where she writes and creates artwork in her attic studio. She earned a BFA in illustration and digital media from Kendall College of Art & Design.

Candace has won many awards in juried shows and contests. She has also worked with a wide variety of clients and collaborators. You can visit her at www.camlingstudio.com